Dedicated to

Mary Jean who has

Allowed me to evolve as

I am – warts and all

They say, best men are moulded out of faults,

And, for the most, become much more the better

For being a little bad

William Shakespeare,

Measure to Measure, Act V Scene 1

I Am Dayo

Winter lasts about three months in this small town. But it is cold and it darkens the spirit. This community is rather tightly sown together. It's a town where everyone pretty much knows everyone and where very few secrets, if any, are successfully kept. And while that's pretty much true about most towns this size, it is especially true of this town. It seems that winter lends itself more to gossip and of the negative sort, more than not. It is easier to turn an evil and dark eye towards a neighbour at eight below than it is at eight above. And it is easier yet, in February than in September. Right now it's about ten below and it's the third week of February.

Christopher Connelly was blowing a thick fog of cold breath over his backyard as he took a brief rest from wailing away at full pieces of wood with an axe. At fifty-three years old, it was becoming quite obvious to Chris that after twenty-five years of practicing law, he was out of shape. Finally, he decided that he had enough wood and so he piled the wood against the side of his house and then took six or seven pieces into his house for his fireplace. He was trying to get all of his chores done for the day, as quickly as possible, because his niece, and goddaughter, was going into the local hospital to be induced. Chris was upset with his niece, Shelley, when she first announced her pregnancy because she wasn't married, had no plans to get married, and wouldn't tell anyone who the father of her child was. He now felt that he was over that and could enjoy the birth of his favourite niece's child. Chris has always been very close to Shelley and took his role as godfather very seriously.

At two-thirty-five, on the afternoon of February twenty-second, Shelley gave birth to a seven-pound, nine-ounce boy. Chris stood around Shelley's bed with her mother and father and her brother when the new baby was brought into the room. Upon seeing the new baby boy, Chris's eyes immediately diverted to the rest of the entourage in an attempt to gage their response, if any was noticeable. There was a brief pause and it was very brief, until

Shelley's mother and father began doting over the newborn. Chris stared at the baby with disbelief. It was clear and absolute that the child was African...Negro...black. There was no doubt. Chris remained silent and eventually joined the family, although mildly and half-heartedly, in their celebration of the blessed event.

Chris arrived home late in the afternoon. Living alone, he had no one to talk with concerning this craziness. Having lost his wife to cancer three years earlier and his daughter, a two-hour airplane ride away at school, he lived a solitary life in his small bungalow. Chris was well respected among his own circle of friends in town. He had, however, developed some detractors, over the years, just as anyone else in a town this size would.

'Just what I need,' he thought to himself, 'a *coon* in the family! What in Christ has she done to herself, her family...everyone? The guys at the club will be going *snaky* over this when they find out. Jesus, how stupid could she be?'

"Good Christ, Evan, she's your daughter," Chris was certainly animated, "and you are my brother. How did this happen? You had no idea?"

"Alright, just calm down." Chris's younger brother Evan was calm and less animated. "This situation is clearly less than ideal, but it is what it is and she is twenty years old and made this decision. We, all of us, are going to have to make the best of it. Hell Chris, it's not the kids fault he's black."

"Are you kidding? You'll be the laughing stock of this town. Do you have any idea what the guys at the club are going to think about this? Really, I don't think you've thought this through at all." Chris noted the pale and distant, blank look on Evan's face.

Chris and Evan were both members of the town's lodge for men. It was a typical men's club where the locals could meet, raise some money for local charities and drink beer together. They would gather on Thursday evenings for some darts, pool and general socializing.

"Can you imagine," Chris was talking with a small group of his cronies at the lodge, "my own niece, goddaughter, with the same last name as me, with a *nigger* son. It's unbelievable."

"Take it easy," one of his buddies whispered, "you may have a point, but in this day and age, if you say that loud enough, you

4

can go to jail. Hell, I could probably go to jail just for standing beside you when you said it."

"Who's the father, that's what I'd like to know?" another crony piped in.

"Yeah, I didn't know we had any in town." The third friend scratched his head.

"Oh, sure, we have a bunch of them. They all live down by the rail yard in those war-time houses." Chris corrected with authority. "I just can't imagine her hanging out with that type, from there."

"So, is she going to keep him?"

"Apparently so," Chris was exacerbated, "she's named him Dayo, which is African, for Christ's sake, for 'joy arrives'. I guess we'll soon see about that."

Evan arrived and joined Chris's group on the far side of the room. "Okay, so who's buying me a beer or do I have to do that myself, as usual?"

A quiet blanket fell over the room. A number of members drifted over to Evan in order to wish him congratulations on becoming a grandfather. And so it was for Evan, Chris and the town.

By the time Dayo was nine years old, his grandfather and his uncle Chris were well detached. An embarrassment for both men, they saw little of him. Neither had spent any time with the boy after his second or third birthday. The mere idea of a black grandson or nephew was abhorrent to their upbringing, their town and their friends. It was easier just not to see Dayo or speak of him. In this way they felt that he was, somehow, invisible...he just never happened!

Dayo's first brush with the law occurred when he was thirteen years old. He was caught by a local storekeeper stealing several music CD's from his store. Of course, his mother turned to her father for help. Evan was not all that happy about being involved. In fact, he truly didn't know what to do or how he could help. His daughter had been an active drug user, usually cocaine, and backed the drug habit up with drinking binges. In desperation and frustration, Evan turned to his brother for guidance.

"Jesus Christ, Chris, what the hell can I do?" Evan was truly animated. "I don't really know this kid. I'm too old for this kind of crap. His mother needs to be a mother instead of dumping all of her problems on everyone else."

"Well look, Evan, I'm sixty-six years old and I know this bastard even less than you do. What are you expecting of me?"

"Well, I thought that you might be more objective being more detached from this kid than I am. You know, maybe you could tell him how he's got to shape up, at least for the sake of his mother. What do you think?"

Chris agreed to speak to Dayo, but by the time he arrived at the ramshackle apartment, in the worst part of town, the police had already dropped the charges as Dayo returned the stolen CDs.

The apartment was filthy, with dirty clothes everywhere, dirty dishes on the table and all over the kitchen. Chris introduced himself.

"Where's your mother, kid?" Chris was direct and icy.

"She's down the street." Dayo looked deeply into Chris's eyes with a cold, calculated stare. 'Down the street' meant the Alpine House Tavern, one of the worst bars in town, where anything can be had for a price.

"Okay, *shit-for-brains,* sit down, I don't won't to hear of any more problems with the police. Do you understand?"

"Hey, *Uncle Brainless,* you don't get to tell me anything, so *go to hell!*" The defiance was dark.

Grabbing the front of Dayo's shirt and pulling it tight under his chin, "Don't you ever use that tone or that kind of language with me again," Chris gritted his teeth as the veins in his own neck bulged. "you got that, hotshot!"

"You ever touch me again, mister and I'll call the police and have you charged." Each of Dayo's words was encased in ice.

"Even at thirteen, you know all the angles, eh boy?"

"My name is not 'boy' any more than yours is 'man'."

Chris released his grip, turned and left.

Dayo had become the pariah of the town. It seemed that no one ever came to his defence or had anything good to say of him. And so it went, month after month, year after year. The town was simply not the place for him to evolve. The male population had completely abandoned Dayo. His father never surfaced, his grandfather was embarrassed by him, while the others despised him. The true irony was his involvement in school. He missed many classes and the school authorities were constantly handing out punishments or trying to. But, in spite of his frequent absences, his school work was above average. He seemed, in some aspects, more mature than his age group. He had also developed a toughened exterior and did not deal well with his many adversaries. He never passed over an opportunity to confront his adversaries face to face, unafraid, or so it seemed.

Chris would forget about Dayo's problems moments after he left.

Dayo continued to evolve with difficulty. He was a teenager with many angles. Some of them sharp and dark and others indicating progress and growth. His schooling actually improved along with his attendance. His social life, however, was heading in the wrong direction. As a strong-willed young man, he was somewhat attracted to the 'gang life' amongst his peers. This dichotomy was a source of great frustration for his teachers and his friends at school. Dayo's obvious intelligence and maturity seemed in absolute contrast with his willingness to take part in activities that could only put his future at risk. Although he had not taken part, personally, in any criminal activities since the stolen CD incident, he did 'hang out' with a gang of black men, most of which were slightly older than he.

"I don't know why I should be concerned about that kid, especially after the way he talked to me." Chris was dismissive.

"Yeah," his grandfather piped in. "he's an asshole."

It was late afternoon, a month after Dayo's fifteenth birthday, as he was standing in front of the downtown branch of the Credit Union. Dayo had agreed to *stand watch* while two or three of his buddies went into the bank and try to cash a *phony* cheque. Dayo agreed to stand outside the bank and in the case of the whole deal going wrong, he would *run interference* outside the bank. Dayo was originally reluctant to get involved on this Saturday morning because he was expected at the gymnasium at his school to help with some younger kids with basketball. He had, however, not spent a lot of time with his *brothers* lately. Dayo was, slowly, if not consciously, drawing down his time with them. His marks at school remained impressive and he was now very involved in the basketball program. He was a leading player for the school's senior team and was helping with younger kids on weekends.

Dayo was asked to be ready, outside the bank, in the event that it went wrong and his buddies came running out of the bank. He was to *block* any bank officials that came running out after his buddies. Dayo didn't think it was much of 'big deal'. They had done this cheque cashing deal before and had never had a problem.

Suddenly, the crack of gunfire from within the bank startled Dayo. At first, he thought that it was a back-fire from a car, but quickly came to the correct conclusion that it was directly connected to the bank and his buddies. A second shot cracked the morning quiet and pulled Dayo around to wait for the aftermath. He stood in shock, staring at the front door of the bank. Waiting! For either his buddies to come screaming out or some employees that he could intercept, protecting his buddy's getaways.

A crowd had gathered in a sort of semi-circle outside of the bank and there were a number of people scurrying around in a fury of activity, when someone grabbed Dayo by his left arm, first, and then almost immediately, his right arm. His wrists were pulled behind his back and shackled with a pair of police handcuffs. The two policemen, one at each arm were both talking to Dayo, but in the maize of the noisy crowd and both officers talking at the same time, he was unable to hear anyone clearly.

"Let's go chump," Dayo could finally make out one of the policeman, "you can join your friends later." The officer then read him his rights and explained, in no uncertain terms, his arrest for bank robbery.

Sitting in a small, square and sweltering hot room at the police station, Dayo was irritated, confused and uncomfortable staring into the cold dark eyes of police detective Banion.

"Okay, kiddo, here's the deal. You know who had the gun. You testify that this Packo kid was the one and you can do twenty easy months in juvenile instead of being tried as an adult and getting twenty-five to life for murder." A sneer laid across the detectives lips. "So what's it going to be *bucko?*"

"Look, I've told you. I was told and I thought it was just a cheque cashing scam. I didn't know that anyone had a gun and so I don't know who had the gun." Trying to appear confident, Dayo could feel the four walls of the room moving in on him. The room was getting smaller and smaller.

"Well, boy, that's unfortunate. For you, that is, unfortunate for you."

After a couple of weeks of negotiations with Dayo, the police could get nowhere with him. Dayo continued to refuse to name anyone in the matter of the gun.

During the time that Dayo had waited outside the bank in order to 'run interference', his buddies were inside attempting a robbery. They told Dayo that they were going to try to cash an illegal cheque because he had, earlier, stated that he wanted nothing to do with any guns, robberies or worse.

Once inside the bank, they approached a teller and told her that they had a gun and that she was to begin stuffing all of her cash in to a plastic bag. The teller immediately set the silent alarm to the police and her bank manager when she hit a key on her computer which also opened her cash drawer. The bank manager left his office and quietly and calmly approached the teller where the two young men were, nervously standing. As the manager approached, the young man with the gun panicked and raised the gun at the bank manager and fired. The gruesome, grey bullet smashed through the man's chest, throwing him to the floor. Piercing his heart, he died instantly. The young man, still in a panic, fired the gun at the ceiling in an attempt to get the attention of the crowd in the bank. At this very moment the police had arrived via the back door of the bank and entered the public area, in force. With guns drawn and pointed at the two young men, they forced them to drop their weapon to the ground and were taken into custody. At the very same moment, Dayo was arrested outside the bank.

Dayo remained adamant with the police that he was not aware that they were going to rob the bank and that they had a gun. The police, of course, did not believe him and ended up charging him with conspiracy to commit murder and were successful, due, in part, to a public outcry, to have him charged and tried as an adult. If found guilty, his sentence could be as long as twenty-five years to life with no chance of parole for fifteen years.

Shelley was crying, uncontrollably, "Couldn't you just listen to him? Jesus, his father is gone, his grandfather pretends that he doesn't exist and his godfather hates him. Why do you hate him?" Tears were streaming down her face and when she finished speaking her lower lip quivered like an inch-worm moving across the floor.

Chris looked at her red swollen eyes. "I don't hate him. Look what's he doing involved in a bank robbery and bloody murder?"

"I told you, he didn't know that they were going to rob the bank and he didn't know that they had a gun. "

"Oh, and after all that he's been up to all of his life, you expect me to believe that"

"So tell me, Uncle Chris," Shelley started out softly, but build to a crescendo, "just what has he done that warrants no help from anyone when he is falsely accused and being mistreated just because he is black?"

Chris froze for a moment, "not the black-card, again."

"That's unfair, he has never called for any special attention because he's black and you haven't answered my question."

Chris stared into her dark, sad eyes. She was right, he thought. Dayo had done nothing to him other than show disrespect for his inattention, lack of help, and lack of love.

"You're right, Shelley. I guess I have been looking on the wrong side of this thing. Maybe right from the start. I guess that I let other's fears and foibles affect my own judgement. I think, as a lawyer, I should have known better." He looked, sheepishly, at the floor.

"Well, here's your chance to do something about it. Look, I've been sober for three weeks, but I don't know what I can do for him. Will you help him, Chris?"

"What the Christ are you doing?" Evan was animated. "This kid is going to cause you nothing but trouble. You know that, Chris. What do you think you can do for this black bastard?"

"Okay, Evan, just take it easy. Jesus! You're his grandfather. Don't you think he deserves a little support from you?" Chris remained calm, but to the point.

"Well, I may be his grandfather, but I'm not like him. I won't be sucked in by him."

Chris fixed his eyes on Evan. There faces were two feet apart, eyeball to eyeball. "You may not be like him. If you took the time to know him you might wish that you were more like him. Look, I'm not suggesting that I have been any better, but after talking with Shelley and taking a good look at myself and my reaction to Dayo over the years it has become clear to me that he deserves our support. You're his grandfather. I'm his godfather. I am Dayo. We are all Dayo. We have all suffered the injustice of being considered at fault when we weren't. We have all struggled to find our true selves, at some

16

time of our lives. His struggle has been made more difficult by our inattention and intolerance. You are Dayo and I am Dayo.

The court room was stark. There were a mere four or five people in the spectator seating. A single prosecutor sat at a table to the judges left. Dayo and Chris sat to the prosecutor's left at a small table. The charges had been read.

"How does the defendant plead?" asked the Judge in monotone.

Rising from his chair, "Not guilty" Chris proclaimed with his head held high.

Mackenzie's Secret

It was the first time that I had found a dead body. It was not the first time that I viewed a dead body, but the first time that I had found a dead body. I was behind the faculty lounge at Mackenzie University and yes, I was about to take a leak. I had been imbibing in a couple of pints of Guinness with an old friend who was also a professor at this dungeon of a college. I needed desperately to pee and was tired of the conversation among a group of self-important, elitist college *Profs* and wandered outside to relieve myself. It was dark and a ten foot path running behind the building turned into a wooded area leading down a hill into a ravine. I wanted, of course, to delve into the wooded area slightly, so as to give myself some cover during my nasty deed. Ten or twelve feet into the wooded area I noticed the glow of a white *slab*. Gently lowering myself down the slight incline of dead leaves and tree branches, the white *slab* began to take shape. Finally, to my horror, it became clear to me that I was a mere couple of feet away from a human body. Naked, it was also clear that it was a female. She was young, probably in her late teens or early twenties. Slowly backing up the incline I found my way to the front of the building where I called 911 on my cell phone and told the police of my disgusting find.

"And you are who?" barked detective sergeant Gus Salvatore.

"I'm Alexander Scott." I bounced back, "your buddy here, detective sergeant Petrovic knows me. Christ, are there no white men on this police force?"

"Watch your mouth, here Scottie," Jim Petrovic smiled, "we're trying to do our jobs. Okay?" Turning to Salvatore, "He's the guy that found the body and called it in."

"And what is your connection to the college here, Scottie?" Salvatore wasn't smiling.

"My only connection here is that I am the world's greatest freelance editor and I was just having a beer with a small collection of the staff here, trying to drum up some business. And this is a university, not a college. And, detective, you are?"

"I'm Gus Salvatore, but you can call me detective sergeant Salvatore."

Let the games begin. This seemed like a perfect beginning to a whole lot of fun. These guys haven't been here for ten minutes, and they have already pissed-off the lead witness in a murder case. I may have to solve this thing for these guys. All kidding aside, this is pretty gruesome for me. Her body was completely naked and no sign of her clothes. That seems very strange to me. The police have cleared me, thank God.

"Look, Scottie, I never professed to be perfect. I have, as we all do, many faults. Unfortunately, my affection for this young girl is...was one of them."

Professor Ryan Randall, or 'R-squared', as I called him, was basically a good guy. I liked going drinking with him from time to time. He'd even given me a couple of editing jobs over the last few years. He was one of these good-looking guys and, yes, he liked the ladies. And it is true that he liked younger ladies. He is in his early forties and likes girls in their very early twenties. Look, everyone is different. I tend to like girls my own age or even older. Then, again, I'm not married and professor 'R-squared' is married. Like he says, 'nobody's perfect'.

"Well, look Ry, I wouldn't be going around bragging about that too much. Have the police been to see you yet?"

"No, not yet. Why would they come see me? They would have no idea that I was seeing this girl." You could hear the worry in his voice.

"Gee, Ry, I think everyone on this campus knew you were seeing her. That's not something that can be kept quiet. They will come to see you, soon enough. Just how deep were you? I mean, you weren't getting too serious or anything, were you?"

"No, no, I was just having some fun. I gave her a necklace awhile ago, but it wasn't much. It was just sixty bucks, or so. It was just a little silver heart thing, nothing serious."

"When did you last see her?" I was deliberate but still friendly.

"About three hours before you found her. Geez, she would come up to the office here when we felt the way was clear. You know, we'd have some wine and then, if time permitted, we'd, you know." Ryan was flushed with embarrassment. "Goddamit, you're right, though, even the gal that works in my office tried to convince me that this little fling was somehow going to cost me."

The dead girls' name was Nancy Tasker. She was very cute, twenty-one and deserved to live a whole lot longer. She had been seeing my friendly professor, romantically, for five months. She was, of course, in one of his classes. This sort of thing was not that uncommon at good ol' Mackenzie University. Too many male professors had been indulging themselves in the fine art of satisfying their animal needs on the backs, so to speak, of the local student body.

"Hey, Detective Salvatore, you out trolling for suspects on this fine sunny day?" I wasn't going to miss a chance to ride this aging Italian.

"Well, Scott, what are you doing here, looking for someone to look up to?" Smiled Salvatore. "Actually, I'm on my way to see your good friend Mr. Randall."

"Do you have a reason to suspect Professor Randall?"

"Do you mean, other than the fact that the good teacher was sleeping with our victim?" I suppose that you could say that Salvatore won this round.

"Yeah, well, have a good day detective."

Well, it's been three weeks, but the jury is in. Ryan Randall's DNA has matched up with that of the trace findings of semen on young Nancy's body. That proves that they had sex sometime, shortly before her death. This was not good. There were no signs of rape or anything like that. Her death was caused by a massive blow to the right back of her head. Two blows at the most and they were both at the same point. No clothes, no weapon and no rape, this was a real strange one. Why would whoever did this remove all of her clothes and why would they remove them from the scene of the crime. The weapon, whatever it was, I understand, but her clothes?

Detective Salvatore was greeted at Professor Randall's office by Candy Sutton. Candy was the professor's receptionist and all around 'girl Friday'.

"My name is Detective Salvatore. May I speak with Professor Ryan Randall, please?"

"He just finished a lecture and is due back any moment. Would you like to have a seat and wait?"

"That would be fine. Have you known the good professor for a long time, Ms...?"

"Sutton, Candy Sutton and yes, I've worked for Professor Randall for about six years now." She was courteous and professional.

"Good guy to work for, is he?"

"Oh yes, he is very nice. All the students just love him and he's always helping someone out, whether it is a student, staff or a fellow teacher."

"Did you know Nancy Tasker, very well?"

"Well, I knew her as a student, you know, I don't think that I could say that I knew her well. I just knew her as one of his students, that's all. I knew that she had a boyfriend and all, but not much else, at least not about her personally."

"She had a boyfriend? Do you know his name?"

"Well, I shouldn't have said that, actually. There was a boy who sure wanted to be her boyfriend, but she kept giving him a hard time. You know, she was not as interested in him as he was in her. His name is Alan Donnelly. A bit of an oddball, but he sure did pursue her 'big time'. She must have turned him down a dozen times, but he kept coming back for more. Real persistent, he was."

"Well, you seem to know quite a bit about this romantic failure."

"Everyone on campus knows about Alan and Nancy. It's sort of legendary."

At that moment, Professor Randall came strolling into the anti-office.

"Professor Randall, I'm Detective Salvatore. May I speak with you, privately for a moment?"

"Yes detective, come right in." He directed the detective into his private office and closed the door.

Detective Salvatore moved about the office like a referee in a boxing match. He remained standing so that the professor might remain standing. It was an old trick to keep the person being questioned from getting too comfortable.

"Have a seat detective."

"Oh thanks, I'm fine." Salvatore began to move ever so slowly behind the two chairs in front of the professor's desk.

Randall remained standing, "How can I help you, detective?"

"I am investigating Ms. Tasker's death and it has come to my attention that you were romantically involved with her. Is that correct?"

"Well, it depends on your definition of romantic." Randall was clearly shaken as he sputtered out the words.

"Let's put it another way, then, professor. You were sleeping with her." It wasn't a real question and it was not put as a real question. It was put as a statement of fact, simply waiting for a 'yes' or 'no'.

"Yes, yes I was, for about five months, now."

Salvatore looked at a spot on Randall's desk, purposely avoiding his eyes, "Do you remember the last time that you had sex with Ms. Tasker?"

It was like getting hit right between the eyes with a line-drive off of a baseball bat. Randall finally realized that he was a serious suspect and it was beginning to look very bad for him.

"Actually, it was about six-thirty on the same day that she died." He felt like he had just run three miles. Randall could feel the beads of perspiration forming on his forehead. He felt queasy and very unsure of himself.

"Where abouts did this take place?"

"Yes, well, it was right here in this office, on that two-seater couch." Randall was pointing to the green couch up against the far wall of his office.

"Professor Randall, how sure are you on that time, six-thirty?"

"I am very sure. I had a lecture between four and six. We often met here right after that lecture."

"And where were you between eight-thirty and nine-thirty that same evening?" Salvatore was direct but not unfriendly.

"Nancy left here at about seven-thirty, quarter to eight and I showered down in the gym facility. I came back up here by about a quarter to nine and marked papers until ten or so and went home."

"Anyone see you during the time between eight-thirty to nine-thirty?"

"What, I'm a suspect?"

"Come on professor, you were screwing her, you're married and she was murdered. Yes you're a suspect, what do ya' think?"

"Okay, sure, there was Professor Daniels who was in the change room as I was getting undressed for my shower. We talked for a minute or so. It had to be after eight o'clock. Then there was a group of students, I knew most of them. They were getting ready for some basketball as I was towelling off and getting my clothes on. I can give you several of their names. That had to be after eight-thirty."

Salvatore's heart sank. The gymnasium facility is quite a ways in the back area of the campus and the faculty lounge was at the very front and a very difficult distance to travel in that short period of time. Besides, he knew that the witnesses were going to check out and he knew in his heart that this professor was no murderer. He was a marriage cheat, but no murderer.

"Okay, professor, I hope that I wasn't too abrupt with you. I have to do my job and my job requires that I am thorough. I hope that you understand."

Detective Salvatore resigned himself to the fact that the only remaining suspect was Alan Donnelly. He needed better luck with Mr. Donnelly than he had with Professor Randall.

The sun was drenching the court yard with light as Detective Salvatore sat on a bench beside Alan Donnelly and chatted with him.

"So someone told me that you were very interested in Nancy Tasker, romantically, I mean."

"And I suppose that someone also told you that I was a screw-ball. That's all a bunch of bull-shit!"

"Actually, it was 'odd-ball' not 'screw-ball' and whether that's bull-shit or not, I need to get some answers to some questions from you."

This kid was sharper than Salvatore had imagined him to be. And while unexpected, it was, in a way, a good sign. Often perpetrators of this kind of crime are very intelligent, often above average. He thought that he better take the offensive before 'bright boy' here, got the upper hand.

"Can you explain your exact whereabouts between eight-thirty and nine-thirty on the twelfth?" Salvatore stared him down the best he could.

"Yeah, I can tell you that, as soon as I am accompanied by a lawyer." The arrogance was absolutely creamy.

"Fine, you got one? Because, if so, we will take you to the station where you can call him and we can all wait there. Me in my office and you in a cell, shall we be on our way Mr. Donnelly?"

"So I'm a suspect?"

"Well, that would have been determined by your answers to my questions. Anyway, we can determine that later."

"Alright, I'll waive my rights to have my lawyer here, if it will get this thing moving."

I'd been drinking with my professor buddies again, playing poker and trying to drum-up some editing work. I stepped outside of the faculty lounge to have a cigarette. Professor Randall decided to join me outside.

"I talked with Salvatore again today," Ryan sounded a bit nervous or maybe it was the sound of solid curiosity.

"What did he have to say?"

"Well, we were talking about her being left naked and no signs of her clothes. I told him about the necklace that I gave her and how she always wore it. Then he told me a strange thing. The necklace wasn't there."

"That could just mean that whoever did this thing stole it."

"Yeah, but she still had an expensive watch on her wrist. Why would the killer take her cheap necklace and not her expensive watch? I don't get it, naked, but no rape or sex, no clothes, a stolen cheap necklace and he left an expensive watch. This is crazy."

Ryan was right. This didn't make any sense, at all.

"And there's another thing," Ryan was clearly confused. "Candy Sutton, my administrative assistant, you know Candy, well she came into my office yesterday and starts coming on to me like crazy. I couldn't understand what was going on. She was leaning over the front of my desk with this low-cut blouse on and I'm sitting at my desk and she's showing me practically everything she owns. She's suggesting that she and I should go for a drink after work. She says that we could have this drink somewhere off campus so as to be discreet. I don't know what she's talking about and my head is spinning."

"Try to keep calm, Ry, it's just another gal wanting to jump your bones."

Now my head was spinning. This had become wacky as hell. It could just be another gal wanting to jump Ryan's bones, but it seems odd that she would choose such a time. So close to the murder of a girl that Candy must have known was sleeping with the boss. What is it with this guy? They're lined up for this guy and the last time I had a steady girlfriend was during the American Civil War.

"Okay, listen Ry, if Salvatore comes back to see you, let me know, will you?"

I think that I would now like to talk with Alan Donnelly. I don't want to interfere with a murder investigation, mind you, I just have an idea about how I might be able to crack this thing.

I met with Alan at *Mac's*, which is the name of the student pub.

"So you were interested in Nancy Tasker, I hear."

"So who are you and what business is it of yours?" Alan was not the most pleasant young man that I have ever talked to.

"Look, sonny, I'm only trying to help you out. The police consider you their prime suspect and I am trying to figure a few things out. This may help remove you as a suspect." I gave him my best *'don't mess with me'* stare.

"The police already know that I have witnesses to the effect that I was nowhere near the scene of Nancy's murder, so don't bullshit me."

"Yeah, well that's not what they told me this morning." Bullshit is right, I was bluffing like crazy. "I'm a friend of Professor Randall and I am trying to get some information that will clear both you and him."

"So what do you want from me?"

"Do you know if Nancy was seeing anyone?"

"The only one that I knew about was your friend Randall. I knew that this was no good for her. Christ, he was old enough to be her father. And besides, her relationship with him wasn't helping with her grades because of that whore that works for him."

"What whore are you talking about?"

"Candy Sutton, that lady that works for him. Everyone knows that she had the *hots* for your buddy, the professor. And she is one jealous lady. She would pretend to lose assignments that Nancy handed in and I'm sure that she bad-mouthed Nancy to him every chance she got."

I made a couple of pleasantries with Alan while I finished my beer. After he left I pulled out my cell phone and called Ryan.

"You going to be in your office for awhile?" I tried not to sound too animated.

"Yeah, I plan to be here for a couple of hours, why?" Randall's voice was calm.

"I'll be right over there." I hung up the telephone quickly.

I was standing in front of Randall's desk while he sat in his chair looking up at me in disbelief. I had burst into his office and now resting my hands on his desk, I talked quickly and urgently.

"Where you seeing Candy Sutton at the same time that you were seeing Nancy Tasker or did one affair stop before the next one began?"

"Candy works for me. That's the only relationship I have or have ever had with her." His eyes were still fixed on mine. "I know that she would like otherwise. I hear the rumours and she has, from time to time, made certain advances, but I have consistently resisted."

34

"Then why were you so surprised by her advances the other day?"

"Because they were just minor manoeuvres in the past, but this time they were very strong and rather obvious. Besides, I didn't want you to know that she was, you know, that way."

"Do you think that Nancy was seeing anyone else?"

"Well, I don't think that I know for sure, but I don't think so. Where are you going with this?"

"I don't really know. I had this notion that maybe this crime was one born out of jealousy, but," I froze in my shoes, looking down at the scrambled mess on Randall's desk. Among the clutter of pen holders and note pad holders, I suddenly noticed the glint of metal tucked in behind the Post-it note pad and the note pad holder. I reached down and pushing the note pad holder aside I saw a lady's necklace. I picked it up and lo and behold I was looking at a heart-shaped pendant on a light silver chain.

"Is this what I think it is?" I held it out in front of Randall's nose.

"Well, it sure looks like it, but what is it doing there?" Randall appeared to be in a state of shock.

Upon examination it was clear that the clasp was broken.

"She couldn't have left it there. She was nowhere near there. I am pretty sure that she had it on when she left that last night. I particularly noticed that it was sort of in the way, around her neck, you know, before we got dressed."

"Wait a minute. You said something the other day about your girl Candy Sutton standing over your desk and giving you a hard time about Nancy and coming on to you. I was right. This was about jealousy, or, at least, I would bet on that."

Two nights later I am smoking a cigarette outside of the faculty lounge and talking with Randall.

"So, I guess it appears that Ms. Sutton was too jealous to continue to work with you while you gallivanted around with other ladies. The police said that she confessed, totally. She guessed that the necklace that she ripped from the dead Nancy's neck must have fallen off of her neck while she was chewing you out. She waited by the faculty lounge until Nancy came by and enticed her to the back side of the building, at the top of the ravine where she hit her, twice in the head with a broken hockey stick. She then rolled her down the incline where she undressed her to make it look like a rape. She went to the bottom of the ravine and made her way across the creek and buried the hockey stick and her clothes. God, I'm good!"

Ryan and I agreed that he might want to get over his attraction to young students and give his family a try. Again, I was in need of a pee. I decided to hold it in until I went back inside and could use the men's-room. God, I'm good!

Shaking the Tree

'If this is the break in the weather, I must've missed something.' Ronny thought to himself. The wind was now blowing the hard cold rain on a horizontal course that was biting the back of his uncovered head. All of this and it was early April, already.

Ronny was new to the downtown area of the big city, but adapting easily to his new life as a *squeegee* guy. Standing under the expressway overpass, he could hear the runoff of rainwater spewing out of the expressway downspout some fifty feet above his head and to his right. On a good day, Ronny could make himself fifteen to thirty dollars cleaning the windows of passing cars. On a day like this one, he was lucky to make five dollars and that would be the result of sympathy donations from passing motorists.

Ronny had his new life figured out and organized. He lived, rent free, in a men's hostel. He would rise at six o'clock each morning and go to the coffee shop, a mere three doors south of his hostel. Always an early riser in his past life, this habit stuck with him. He enjoyed a cup of coffee and a biscuit each morning. He would then walk the four blocks south to the open area under the expressway where he would *squeegee* cars until noon. Then it was back to the coffee shop for a bowl of soup, a sandwich and a glass of water. After lunch, Ronny would walk the two large blocks west to the main street running north away from the lake. Here, he would panhandle for two hours, or so. On many days, he would make twenty-five dollars or more. Ronny needed about sixteen dollars a day for breakfast, lunch and dinner. Dinner was always at the tavern, nicknamed by Ronny and his friends *'the trough'*. He would indulge in four or five glasses of beer after he ate his dinner. He arrived in town with his total savings of four hundred dollars and on those days when Ronny made less than thirty dollars, he would have to dig into his stash or cut back on his intake of food or drink. Dinner was often sacrificed for beer.

It was eleven o'clock on this wet and windy April day and Ronny had made a total of six dollars. Receiving three *sympathy donations* of two dollars each, he decided to walk back to the coffee shop for an early lunch. He left his friend, Jimmy and two young girls under the expressway and trudged into the onslaught of rain. By the time that he arrived at the coffee shop he was thoroughly wet. Ninety minutes later he had consumed his bowl of soup and a hot cup of coffee and had dried sufficiently to start the trek over to the main street to try some panhandling before dinner.

"You never were one for work, were you?" Dianne's voice was shrill and accusatory. Dianne had been married to Ronny for twenty-two years and she had doubts that she would see their twenty-third anniversary together.

Ronny started drinking heavily during their fifth year and while it was a couple of times a week that he would not arrive home until midnight or after, it was the heavy drinking that was originally of concern. It was two years later that Dianne began to become concerned about whatever else he may be doing until all hours of the morning. And it was now four or five times a week.

"I work every day, unlike you and your teacher friends. You guys are on the 't-t-t-t-t-t' system...Tuesday to Thursday, ten to two.

What do you work? About four hours a day for about five months a year!"

Finally, after twenty-two years of marriage and the last seventeen or so being an emotional wasteland, Dianne kicked him out. Ronny lasted another ten months at his job until he was fired. He was a chartered accountant and the enormous amount of time-lost and poor performance, when he was there, was his undoing. Another eight months drinking his unemployment earnings and driving his savings down to four hundred dollars, Ronny took the plunge and moved an hour and a half up the highway to the big city.

The rain had subsided and over the next two hours, Ronny had accumulated twelve dollars. Suddenly, the rain started again. He had thirteen dollars in one pocket and nine dollars in his other pocket. The nine dollars was the result of some skimping over the past four or five days. The twenty-two dollars was more than enough for dinner, beer and tomorrow's breakfast. It was time to head back to the hostel where he could dry off and lie down for a spell before he ventured over to the 'Trough'.

Walking back in the cold rain, his mind wandered back to one of the last words that his father had spoken.

"If you're not careful, Ronny, you're going to end up all alone with nothing...not a pot to piss in or a window to throw it out of." His father was direct and cold, red-eyed and half drunk. His unshaven face betrayed years of defeat.

Ronny awoke in his room with a start. It was six-fifteen in the evening and he was running late against his usual schedule. He needed a cigarette. His daily routine regarding smoking was to allow himself two cigarettes per day, both to be enjoyed during dinner and beer. With his cigarette pangs circling his head, he rushed to the *'Trough'*. His cronies were already well into their nightly discussion when Ronny arrived.

Ronny was just finishing the last gulp of beer from his first glass when he felt a light tap on his shoulder, from behind. Turning on his barstool, he found himself looking straight into the familiar eyes of a skinny, but attractive female face.

"Hi Ronny." It was one of the girls that hung around the squeegee area in the mornings. Sheila Williams was a twenty-eight year-old who had been on the streets for twelve years. Standing beside her was her constant companion, Sonja Magnuson. Sonja was twenty-two and had been on the streets since she was eighteen.

"Hey, Sheila, Sonja, *whattayasay?*"

Sonja immediately turned her attention to the middle-aged crony sitting beside Ronny. Ronny turned to his crony and asked him to move down a couple of stools so Sheila and Sonja could sit down. Sonja sat beside the crony while Sheila sat by Ronny.

Ronny could overhear Sonja's conversation two stools down from him.

"So you want some company?" She was leaning well into his friend's face at this point.

"Sheila, why do you guys do that? Can't you find some other way to get by?" Ronny's half smile betrayed the seriousness of his comment.

"*Look,* Sonja and I both come from fathers who loved us. They loved us a lot. They loved us often and ever since we were old enough to play in the dirt. So don't give me any of your shit! What are you, a model of high society, or something?"

"Hey, alright, I'm simply concerned. That's a dangerous business and I wouldn't want either one of you to get hurt." Ronny's concern was genuine.

"I appreciate that Ronny. Look, if I can do something for you sometime, you let me know. I know this is dangerous. I'm cutting back quite a bit, myself. I try to keep an eye on Sonja and her activities, but we both need the money. I have been able to cut back my cocaine use, but Sonja is having some problems in that area. It's going to take her some time."

Sheila turned her attention to Sonja.

"Hey girl, work day is over. Let's go. Just relax."

Sonja's eyes glazed over and were merely half-open. It was, surely, time to go.

The two girls said goodnight to Ronny and left the tavern. Ronny turned on his barstool and focused on his last glass of beer for the night.

Ronny's walk back to the hostel was taken up with memories of his good friend, Niles Tandy. The memory was still intact of years of working with Niles and keeping in touch even after Ronny had lost his job and his marriage. The details had become a little fuzzy, but the gist of it was still filed away and recoverable. Those many years were always looked back at with a sense of delight. He had not heard from Niles since his move to the big city, but he was sure that he would. As far as Ronny knew, Niles was still working as an executive at the hotel supply company that Ronny had once worked as the Chief Accountant. Of course, that was now a hundred years ago. Two downgraded jobs later and now he was the *Prince of Squeegee*. It had been an incredible journey.

The third week in May brought with it the first genuine break in the weather. Mid afternoon on Saturday and Ronny was on his second glass of beer in the *'Trough'*. Sheila was sitting beside him on a barstool. They had become fast friends over the five or six weeks since their first conversation in the tavern.

"Hey Ronny, how come you never hit on me? Don't you find me attractive?"

Ronny was somewhat taken aback by her blurted question, even with her toothy smile.

"I can't afford you." He lowered his head in order to hide the half-smile.

"Come on, I don't mean that way. I have regular feelings and regular needs like any other girl, ya' know."

"I suppose I'm your tree shaker, right?"

"My tree shaker? What the hell is that all about?"

Ronny's smile now covered the breadth of his face.

"That's a quote from a famous German philosopher name Nietzsche about heroes. Don't worry about it."

Sheila's face lit up with enthusiasm.

"No, tell me or I'll stick my finger in your beer."

"Yeah, you would. It's just a couple of lines, it goes, *'Here is a hero who did nothing but shake the tree as soon as the fruit was ripe. Does this seem to be too small a thing to you? Then take a good look at the tree he shook'.* I used to read a lot of deep shit like that."

"So, you want to be my hero?"

"I'm afraid I've never been anyone's hero. I'm not the hero type, I guess."

"Like I said, how come you never hit on me?"

"Well, I like you fine. You're a nice person and very attractive. But I don't think that you would want to get involved with a bum like me, not that way, anyhow."

"Well, I might surprise you. Give it a shot, some time."

"So where's Sonja?" He avoided direct eye contact.

"Oh, she's with this guy from uptown. Some executive type, I guess. A real asshole, if you ask me." Her comment was caustic in sound and body language.

"If he's an asshole, why does she see him? What's his name, anyway?"

"I don't know. I think he's giving her 'crack'. But I don't know all he's getting for it, if you know what I mean. I saw his name on a business card attached to his briefcase in his car. His first name is Justin, but I couldn't see the last name so good."

"Jesus, that doesn't sound so great." Ronny was genuinely concerned.

"Yeah, well, I'll see what I can learn from her when I see her. So what have you got planned for the day?"

"Nothing special, I've got some money if you want to hang around. We could eat together later, if you like."

"Sounds like fun." Her smile was a mile wide.

"My best friend is coming to visit me next weekend. You should meet him. He's a big-shot with the company that I used to work for. Great guy, he gave me some money when I needed it back then, wouldn't let me pay him back, either. We sure had a lot of great times together. Anyway, you should meet him next week." Ronny's voice seemed to drift off. He wasn't sure why he told Sheila about Niles, except that if Niles met her, he might think that he was doing okay

"So what kind of great times did you have with this Niles guy?"

"Well, mostly drinking, we used to party at the local pub two or three times a week."

"Well, it's nice to have one good friend. That's why I cling so close to Sonja."

"Yeah, it's nice."

Ronny and Sheila drank steadily through to five-thirty. Neither of them was in the mood for any food, so they retired to Sheila's place where they made love. It was Ronny's first time in about fifteen months. He slept until two-thirty Sunday morning when he rose with a hangover and quietly left while Sheila remained asleep. The twenty minute walk back to his hostel did nothing for his headache.

Lying in bed at the hostel, it occurred to Ronny that Sonja was not at home with Sheila when he left. He promised to remind himself to ask Sheila about her when they next saw each other.

It had been three days since Ronny's Sunday hangover. He hadn't made any money to speak of during that three-day period. He stayed at home all day Monday. On Tuesday, he tried some squeegee work but lasted only an hour and a half, making four dollars. Today, Wednesday, he was under the expressway and anxious to make some money.

Ronny was reminded of one of his father's all too frequent verbal lashings.

"You'll never amount to anything. You're weak and a sissy. You need to grow up and grow up fast, mister." *His father was*

staggering, side to side as he ranted. The odour of alcohol on his breath was pungent.

Twenty minutes after Ronny arrived at the *'Trough'*, the sky darkened and rain appeared to be imminent. Gradually, his mood darkened with the sky as the rain began. He had been digging into his stash for days and a mild panic started to take hold of him.

Ronny sat at his usual bar stool and stared, solemnly, straight ahead at the mirror with its skyline of bottles of cheap scotch, rye, rum and gin. Suddenly, Sheila sat beside him.

"Hi, kiddo," Ronny smiled, "where's Sonja?"

"Well, she came home Sunday night. She'd been doing crack all weekend. Apparently, she stayed with this guy Justin in the Four Seasons all weekend. God knows what he gave her or what she had to do for it. Anyway, she was a bit upset and then she left Monday night and I haven't been able to find her, since." Sheila's calm demeanour betrayed a sense of urgency and mild panic.

"That doesn't sound too good. You know anything more about this guy?" Ronny took a long, deep breath.

"Yeah, well, I found a business card on the floor of the bedroom. His name is Justin Langstaff. He's some kind of big shot with PHG Insurance. He looks pretty young for a vice president."

"PHG!" Ronny exclaimed, "They're pretty big. Must be some kind of pervert."

"What?" Sheila was suddenly, hopping mad. "Just because he pays for it? What are you, one of the disciples?"

"Lookit, I just think that a young guy like that, using drugs to have sex with a girl like Sonja is just a little unusual...morally speaking"

"Well, morals can be a little unusual, so to speak."

"Well, we better try to find Sonja, if you ask me." Ronny was exacerbated.

"Yeah, you're right there." Sheila downed the remaining beer in her glass.

Niles had arrived at 2:30 pm on Saturday afternoon. He met Ronny at the "Trough". After twenty minutes, or so of catching up, Niles turned to Ronny.

"Will you, at least, take some money? Just as a loan, you understand."

"No, I'm fine, really. I'm getting by and I couldn't take your money. You have already done your share to help me. I'm okay."

"Okay, but if you need some later, I hope you'll let me know. Have you met anyone? Made any friends, yet?"

"Well, yeah, I have met this girl, Sheila."

"So, you living with this girl?"

"No, no, we're just good friends. She sort of baby-sits this Sonja girl and I kind of help out."

"Help her what? How old is this Sonja?"

"Well, she's in her twenties, but she has some problems. Don't worry about it."

Just then, Sheila burst through the doors of the tavern and raced to Ronny's side.

"They found Sonja!" She was breathing heavily and short of breath.

"Hey, calm down. They found her where? What are you talking about?"

Sheila quickly caught her breath and lowered her voice to a whisper. "They found Sonja in an alley about five blocks north of here. She's dead!" Heavy tears welled-up in Sheila's eyes. She began to sob slowly and quietly as she buried her face in Ronny's shoulder.

"Holy Christ!" Ronny whispered as he put his arm around Sheila.

Niles looked at Ronny in disbelief. 'What the hell has Ronny got himself into?' he wondered.

It had been three weeks since Sonja was found dead of an overdose of 'crack' cocaine. At least, that's what the authorities said. Sheila had scarcely mentioned Sonja's death until now.

"That bastard did it. He should pay for this."

"What do you mean?" Ronny spoke softly, "what bastard and how do you know?"

"That bastard Langstaff. That Justin guy who was feeding Sonja's habit for whatever. I just talked to him."

Ronny was confused. The buzz from the beer or maybe it was just his normal state of mind after working the streets in the big city for a few months.

"You just talked to him? Where? What are you talking about?" Ronny could feel the first stages of a panic setting in and its unpleasant companion...fear.

"I was under the expressway. You know, where we always go. This fancy car pulls up and I look in." Tears stream down Sheila's face as her lower lip begins to quiver. "I notice, right off, that it's this guy Justin, the big shot with PHB. He asks me if he can get some company. So I said that I wasn't interested. He says that he can make it worth my while with lots of cash or 'crack'. I don't like his mouth, so I tell him to go screw himself." Her hands were now shaking every bit as much as her lower lip. "He says that if I'm not a little nicer, I get the same as Sonja." Sheila was now inconsolable.

Ronny didn't know what to say. He fumbled in his head for what seemed to be the longest time until he blurted out, "So, with that, this guy takes off?"

"Yeah, he calls me a stupid *'dyke'* and takes off. I'm telling you, this guy killed Sonja."

"Well, what if he heard about Sonja and decided to try to scam you into going with him? Maybe he's just a real prick!"

"Lookit, asshole, Sonja wouldn't overdose. She was too smart and careful for that. This guy did it! I could see it in his eyes and that god-awful smirk of his. Yes, he's a prick, but he's also a bloody maniac. Is nobody going to do anything about this?"

Ronny looked around the tavern. He didn't know what he was looking for, but he looked, anyway.

Suddenly, his thoughts swung back to his father.

Ronny's father was pressing down hard on Ronny's ankle with his left foot and leg. When Ronny stopped wincing, his father looked down at him in disgust.

"You and your stupid books, you don't know what a real man is, just what you see on TV. You'll never know what it feels like to be a real man. You're just a weak little shit."

Ronny gathered his wits about him, momentarily.

"You'll have to go to the police and tell them. I'll go with you."

"Don't be crazy, Ronny. The police aren't going to pay any attention to me. I don't have any evidence. And the police aren't going to bother looking into this because I think that this guy did it. To them I'm just a goddamn hooker and drug addict."

"Okay, okay, just calm down. I'll think of something, just calm down."

He knew that Sonja was neither too smart nor too careful to overdose, but he was also convinced that Sheila had this whole thing figured out.

It was two weeks before Ronny's first Christmas in the big city. His money had run a little low, but if he were careful over the winter, he could get by. Just as he began to stare off into the mirror of the bar directly across from where he sat, Niles came through the door of the tavern and walked over to Ronny.

"Hey, how's she going?" Ronny spread a huge and welcoming smile at Niles.

"Pretty good, *old buddy*, pretty good. I can't stay long. I've got to be up by the airport for six. You need some money?"

"Nope, I'm okay. I might need some through the winter, but I'll let you know."

"Say, how's your girlfriend, Sheila, after what happened to her friend, that Sonja girl? Overdose of drugs, wasn't it?"

"No, I don't think so. Sheila sure doesn't think so, anyway. We're pretty convinced that some insurance big shot, a real prick, might have had something to do with it, name of Justin Langstaff."

"Justin Langstaff!? Isn't that the guy on the news? They found him in the stairwell of his office building. He had been strangled and stabbed in the eye or something. Is it the same guy?"

Ronny looked Niles straight in the eyes, "no, no, I don't think so. This was a different guy."

Just as Niles' eyes began to squint and sharpen in Ronny's direction, Sheila sauntered into the tavern. She moved gracefully over to where Ronny and Niles were sitting. She nestled up to Ronny's side, slid her arm around Ronny's neck and gently kissed him on the cheek and turned to Niles.

"Hi, Niles, what's up?"

When Knights Were Bold

A light misted silhouette rested against a watered down, blue-blanket sky. Thick, white smog exited from a distant smokestack in the late afternoon.

Off in the distance, perhaps a hundred and fifty feet away, Ellis was able to make out a mound of light blue and dark blue fabric. As he approached, it became obvious that the mound was a human. Standing over the still, stark heap, Ellis recognized the uniform of a city policeman. Upon further examination, he decided that the constable had received at least two traumas to the head. There was a clump of blood and an apparent breaking of the skin at the temple area and another at the front hairline of the head. There was no need to examine the body any further. The constable was dead. Ellis could tell by looking at the severity of the two wounds that he was surely dead. Of this, Ellis was certain.

'One more time,' he thought, 'I am called upon, one more time.'

Behind him, Ellis could feel the flashing lights and hear the running motor of a police car. He turned to see the car come to a stop about fifteen feet from where he was standing. The driver opened the door of the cruiser and calmly stepped out and moved toward Ellis.

"Good afternoon, sir."

"Good afternoon, officer."

"What have we here?" The officer remained polite and calm.

"Well sir, I believe we have a dead police constable." Ellis was also calm and spoke in an even, but clear monotone.

"Can you tell me what's happened here?"

Ellis was deliberate, "I was walking along these rail tracks and just now noticed the body. I looked at the two wounds and I can tell you that he is certainly dead."

The officer seemed puzzled, "Did you touch the body in any way, sir? I mean how can you tell that he is dead just by looking at his wounds.?"

"The wounds are severe and he is definitely dead. And no sir, I did not touch the body."

"Okay," a slight smirk came over the officer's lips, "could you stand back a few feet and remain standing there while I check out the situation?"

"Certainly," said Ellis, "can I be of any assistance?"

"No sir, thank you." The officer chuckled, mildly. "If you could just stand back a bit until I am finished."

The officer knelt beside the body and checked the pulse, both at the wrist and the neck. He then removed the dead constable's wallet from his back pocket with a minimum of disturbance to the position and placement of the body.

You're right. He appears to be dead. Is there anything else that you want to tell me about this?"

"I've told you everything that I can. I don't know of anything else that could be of help to you, right now."

"Are you telling me that you have had nothing to do with this?"

"That's correct, officer. I have found this situation as it is, just moments prior to your finding it."

"What did you mean – *'right now'*?"

"I'm sorry?"

"You said that you couldn't help anymore, *'right now'*. Do you anticipate helping sometime in the future?"

"I only meant that if I could be of any help, now or in the future, that I would be only too glad to do so." Ellis remained calm and pleasant.

"What's your name?" the detective's tone was slightly terse.

"Ellis."

"Is that a first name or last name?"

"John, John Ellis. Everyone just calls me Ellis. Always have."

Well, John Ellis, I think that you should accompany me to the station where we can be comfortable and I can ask you some questions. Would that be okay with you, Mr. Ellis?"

"That would be fine, sir."

The officer made the mandatory calls to alert his superiors of the situation and once they arrived, he drove Ellis to the local police station. They arrived at the station at five-fifteen in the afternoon. Ellis found himself in a room that was about fourteen feet square. It had three tables placed beside each other and a large window looking out into the street and the front entrance of the station. It was late June and the bright daylight remained from the late afternoon sun.

The officer questioned Ellis for about ninety minutes. Suddenly, through the door came a taller and slender man in a grey tweed jacket. He was a friendly looking man. He introduced himself.

"Hello, Mr. Ellis, my name is Detective Carl Kadlovski. I am with the homicide department. I would like to ask you a few questions. I won't be long. Is that okay?"

"That would be fine detective. I hope that I can be of help."

Kadlovski immediately found Ellis' tone to be strange, considering the situation.

"Where do you live, Mr. Ellis?"

"I rent a basement apartment in a house just a few blocks from here on Salem Avenue.

And, as I have told your officer, I don't work. I inherited some money some time ago. I am fifty-four years old and I have never been in any trouble with the police."

"Fine, Mr. Ellis, are you married? Any family in town?"

"I've never been married and I have no family. I had no siblings and my parents are dead."

"Look, Mr. Ellis, I'm sorry to be repeating these questions, but this is a very serious situation and I have to be absolutely sure of my information. You do understand, don't you?"

"Yes, of course I do."

Kadlovski arranged for Ellis to leave and asked that he remain available to the police for a few days, in case they needed to talk to him again. It was five minutes after eight in the evening.

After Ellis had left, the officer who first questioned him came into the room.

"How come you let him go? Couldn't you just hold him overnight? What if he bolts on us?"

"What am I going to hold him on? Constable Mallam's wallet had forty-three dollars in it. There are no fingerprints to match up. No weapon and no apparent motive. Just what am I going to hold this guy on?" Kadlovski remained calm and to the point.

"This guy's a little weird, but I don't think he's a cop killer. Knowing Mallam's attitude, I'd be surprised to learn that his killer is a white, Anglo-Saxon Christian with a conservative ideology. What about you?"

"Ya, I guess you're right. Well, the summer of 1959 is only a day old. This will sure heat things up."

Anthony Baca hung up the telephone and turned to the newspaper folded on the top of his desk. His new office was impressive in size. As the newly appointed general manager of Master Edge Limited, Tony is convinced that the next step on the ladder is to become the first president of the company to be of Italian heritage. He felt that he knew more about the manufacture of fine quality kitchen knives than any other Italian, at least, that he knew. At thirty-three years old, he had lived in the city for twenty-four years. He and his parents had left Italy to come to North America in 1935 when Tony was only nine years old. Now he would prove that the city sidewalks were, indeed, paved with gold and he would show all that cared to notice that an Italian immigrant could *make it big*. All it took was determination and hard work.

The headlines in the afternoon newspaper were high and bold. **CITY POLICEMAN MURDERED – NO SUSPECTS – NO LEADS.** The previous day's event took up two thirds of the front page. Constable Ken Mallam was a fifteen-year veteran of the police force. He was born in Birmingham, England and arrived in the city at age twelve. The constable was four days shy of his thirty-fifth birthday when his life ended. He was divorced for eleven years, had no children and with both parents deceased. His only surviving family were numerous cousins, aunts and uncles back in England. It had been a long time since the city had experienced a murdered policeman. The proper disdain for the heinous act was expressed by the senior police officials, the cops on the beat, the city government, the media and the public, at large.

Tony read the latest news about Constable Mallam's demise with more than a passing interest. Mallam was murdered, not far from Tony's home and the policeman was a known fixture in the area as the 'cop on the beat'.

His thoughts turned, now, to getting home for supper and the opportunity to spend some time with nine-year-old son, Paul. Paul was about to finish his school year putting grade four behind him. The major issue in his young life, at this time, was the acquisition of *marbles* for the upcoming *marbles* season in September when he entered grade five. He would be ten years old in October and this was a prime age for *marbles* players. The game would involve the striking of a *marble, allie, aggie, boulder or steely* with another *marble* while it rested on the concrete schoolyard between the legs of a hopeful player. There were other variations involving pieces of wood with holes cut from them for players to attempt to roll a *marble* through in order to 'win' a number of *marbles*. The advantage to the player owning the wooden board was that the player kept all of those *marbles* not entering the holes. The simple acquisition of *marbles* and all of their related pieces was the goal of every player. Bragging rights were inherent with the growing inventory or winning and keeping a particularly unique piece such as a *boulder* – simply, a large *marble*, or a *steely* – a solid steel ball bearing.

Tony Baca was intent on making his son happy. He would do anything to insure that Paul enjoyed all of the positive aspects of his adopted society.

Tony remembered his adventure some two years earlier in the local rail yards. *Steely's* were a particularly prized possession in the world of schoolyard *marbles* and the best way to accumulate *steely's* was to search the rail yards. The ball bearings were used extensively in the wheel assemblies of train wheels. Often, the rail yards would offer up discarded wheels that could be disassembled if they were not already in this state. Eight to fifteen ball bearings could be found in different wheel assemblies. Various sizes could be found and for the purpose, at hand, the larger the better. This was the search that Tony had committed to doing for the sake of his son's contentment and acceptance by the predominately white Anglo-Saxon and mostly English surroundings. This commitment would insure Paul's place in the hierarchy of schoolyard society.

Sunday was the first day of summer and Tony would take full advantage of the bright sunny day to visit the local rail yard in search of ball bearings. It was early afternoon when Tony left the house for the four-block walk to the rail yard. His mood was as high as the blue sky as the he approached the wire fence along the perimeter of the yard. Squeezing through the opening, he entered the forbidden area. Looking around, he noticed an area to his left that appeared to be refuse of unwanted rail debris. There were three or four, what seemed to be, abandoned boxcars and mounds of discarded rail wheels heaped in a mass of rust and grease. Tony wandered into the area. He perused the area for approximately ten minutes before he realized there were no ball bearings lying about. He would have to take some of the discarded wheels apart in order to reap his treasure. Looking about for something that would assist him in removing the back hubs of the wheels, he saw the large wrench, still adhered to the oil pump some twenty feet away. The wrench, about three feet long, was attached to the valve of the oil pump. A maintenance employee mistakenly, no doubt, left it there. This looked, to Tony as an ideal implement to help him with his task. He punched down on the extended end of the wrench and dislodged it from the valve. The wrench was quite heavy. Tony manoeuvred it to the area where the wheels rested, waiting to be hatched for their interior treasure. Using the wrench as leverage, he turned a large wheel over, exposing its backside.

"Hey, *dego!* What do you think you're doing here?"

The English accent was unmistakable and Tony, although startled, knew immediately who was approaching him from behind.

"Officer," Tony remained respectful as he turned to face the police officer, "I'm not doing anything wrong."

"You most certainly are. You *grease-ball whop.* There are 'no-trespassing' signs all up and down this fence. Now, maybe you can't read English, but that's too bad. We got laws here and you and every other *DP* has to abide by them."

Tony was all too familiar with the officer. The cop 'walked the local beat' and Tony had experienced his unpleasant demeanour on four or five occasions over the past year. His son, Paul, had also been on the receiving end of the constable's acid-tongued comments concerning his heritage. The references to *dego, grease-ball whop,* and *DP* were a cause of boiling blood for Tony. He had been driven to the edge of temperamental explosion on more than one occasion. This restraint was, however, increasingly difficult.

"Look, constable, I was just trying to get some ball bearings for my son. These wheels are no good to anyone. I'm not hurting anything of value or anybody." He responded in a pleading tone.

"Is that right, *dego?* Well, I guess you wouldn't understand that the rail people here fix these wheels and other parts. They re-use them in order to save money, which helps all of us. So, I've got you on trespassing and theft, you *whop, son-of-a-bitch.*"

The constable's words and the tone started Tony's head spinning. His eyes blurred and he began to feel as if he were two hundred feet away from the officer, instead of two feet. Slowly, a thumping and grinding headache began. Tony became detached from the very scene in which he was a central figure. He noticed the wrench rising in his hand. But it was not he who was lifting it. His eyes filled with burning tears. He saw the wrench now raised over his head. He saw the slow motion contortion of the officer's face as the wrench slowly descended to the side of the cop's head. Suddenly, the aura of slow motion ended. Tony looked down at the uniformed body. He could see the patch of red blood and tissue of all colours on the side of the head. He must end this abuse. His son would understand. His wife would understand, the authorities would understand. All Italians, everywhere, would praise him for his courage to do the right thing. The second blow was not in slow motion. He struck the officer in the forehead, at the hairline. It took a fraction of a second. His headache remained and it would continue for seven or eight hours.

Tony found an oil-soaked rag and cleaned down the wrench and using the rag to carry the wrench, he crawled under one of the abandoned boxcars and wedged the wrench in the undercarriage of the wheel assembly. He then dragged the body through the opening in the fence and rolled it down the small incline beside the rail yard. The constable rested approximately two feet from the road in some eight to ten inches of grass. Tony left for home. There he could administer aspirin and lay down.

Examining the file on Constable Mallam, Kadlovski heard the tap on his door.

"Mr. Ellis is here and wants to talk to you." The officer shrugged his shoulders as Kadlovski looked up from his desk.

"Well, show the mysterious Mr. Ellis in."

It had been just over forty-eight hours since the discovery of the dead cop's body. Kadlovski was glad to speak to anyone remotely connected to the case. As of this moment he had little, if anything, to go on.

Ellis entered the detective's office. He was offered a chair and sat across the desk from Kadlovski.

"Detective Kadlovski," Ellis was calm and direct, "I believe that I may be able to shed some light on the constable's demise. May I take a moment of your time?"

Ellis' comment sounded very formal. There was something very slightly different about Ellis. He seemed more formal and very self-confident in his tone and appearance. The detective discounted these feelings as soon as he had noted them. They did not, of course, at any rate, matter in the least.

"So Mr. Ellis, what can you tell me?"

"I believe the constable had a bit of a problem with his tolerance level for those people that differed from himself. Would you say that to be true, sir?"

"Well, I've not heard it put quite that way. But yes, Ken Mallam was not the most enlightened guy around here. What of it?"

"It would seem that Constable Mallam targeted a particular gentleman of Italian descent. He provoked this gentleman beyond his breaking point and paid the ultimate punishment for his sin of intolerance."

"Really, well, just how do you come by this information."

There was a pause. It seemed to Kadlovski to last for a summer long-weekend.

"I am rolling thunder," in a voice louder than normal, but not screaming, "assaulting the heavens and the earth as punishment for the broken promises and false hopes."

Kadlovski stared at Ellis in amazement. This comment shot through him like a rush of strong wind speeding through his lungs and out a hole in his back.

"Who the hell are you?" Kadlovski almost whispered.

"Hell, my dear sir, is a concept , more real than any concept of heaven that you may know of. We build this hell, brick by brick, with every breath and every moment. Heaven requires a faith in high structures and flying spirits sold to the highest bidders among us."

"That's all very interesting," the detective was almost in shock, "but you haven't answered my question."

"I am one who helps keep the bricks of hell from getting so high that you cannot see over them."

A quarter of a mile away, Tony Baca stood at the rail crossing, ten feet from the tracks. He stood and stared in silence. Waiting...and waiting. He stood there for approximately ten minutes when he could scarcely hear the low and seemingly distant rumble of an oncoming train. Looking, first to the right and then to the left, he determined that the train was coming from the left. Indeed, he was now able to see the train in the distance. Tony readied himself until the train reached a point about two hundred yards from where he stood. At this point he broke into a run in the direction of the train, but off the tracks trotting parallel to the ongoing locomotive. At a distance of about one hundred feet from the train, Tony sharply veered onto the tracks and ran straight for the mammoth vehicle. With not enough time for the engineer to react, Tony's fate was sealed and his mission had been accomplished.

"I'm sorry, Mr. Ellis," Kadlovski was calm but frustrated, "I don't have any idea what you are saying. I think that you should get some help. Maybe I should take you to the local hospital. I'm sure that they can help you."

Suddenly, a throbbing took over Ellis' skull. An unseen shiver took over his entire body as he broke into a sweat.

"That won't be necessary, detective Kadlovski. Nothing more, on your part, is now needed. Constable Mallam's killer has now paid for his sins. You will not have to pursue him any longer."

"Mr. Ellis, what are you saying? Do you know who killed Mallam?" Kadlovski's voice was louder and betrayed his exacerbation.

"He was a local business man. He had been harassed by the constable for some time and finally broke out at your constable, in a rage. You will find a suicide at the rail tracks near where the policeman's body was found. Both the constable and his killer have now paid for their sins of fear and ambition."

The temperature was somewhere in the high nineties. The street was a cloud of dust. Ellis was well aware that around the corner at the next laneway, he would find a troublesome situation.

'One more time,' he mused to himself, 'I am called upon, one more time.'

This time, he walked near the downtown area of Cairo, Egypt in the summer of 2064.

Winding Up the Sun

Ryan was startled awake by a crashing noise. The alarm clock on the night table read five-twenty-five. Rubbing his bleary eyes, Ryan slowly manoeuvred his feet to the floor and gradually stood. He stretched his arms high above his head, yawning and grunting.

It was a total mystery as to how the five books could have fallen to the floor. Ryan had them stacked neatly on the top of his dresser and not so close to the edge. Nonetheless, there they were, in a collected heap on the floor beside the dresser. The reason seemed obvious when he noticed the window directly opposite his bed was three quarters open. Surely a gust of wind had blown the books off of his dresser.

In his sixteenth year, Ryan was beginning his summer school break on the farm where he was born. His father, Josh Palmer, grew corn, cabbage, cauliflower, lettuce and tomatoes. Ryan was a sensitive teenager, very interested in the world of art. He was an accomplished sculptor and read and wrote poetry. His favourite poet was Lord Byron and he read his work voraciously. His love of the arts was the source of some unspoken tension between his father and himself. Josh's genuine love for Ryan was not in doubt. There was simply an aura of some lack of connection between the two. Josh enjoyed no passion for the arts and had no understanding of them, whatsoever. This chasm, while apparent to most, was never communicated openly. It was simply there and not considered by any to be of major importance. Except, perhaps to Ryan. He had read this situation to be some kind of lack of affection on his father's part and spent much time turning it over in his mind. He would often turn to his mother for the affection that seemed lacking with his father. Amelda Palmer was a loving and strong woman, dedicated to the happiness of her husband and son. At thirty-seven years old, she suffered horrifically from severe arthritis and heart angina. She took every opportunity to assure Ryan that his father loved him dearly and that the lack of open affection was merely a personality trait.

She seemed to understand that Josh's undemonstrative attitude was due, in large part, to his notion of masculinity so unfortunately learned at his own father's knee. She understood that it was not likely to change. However, she also knew that it was never going to diminish his love of his son, regardless of his inability to demonstrate it, openly. For this reason and many others, Ryan was totally devoted to his loving mother and tried, at all times, to alleviate her arthritic and chest pain.

Ryan would recall the crashing book incident some three weeks later when the distinct movement of his bed awakened him. This movement took place while he was asleep. He arose from bed to turn on the light and could plainly see that the bed had, indeed, moved about fifteen inches on an angle away from the wall at the headboard, on the right side. Bewildered, he lay on the floor checking underneath the box spring. What he was looking for, he wasn't sure. After all, an object of this size doesn't move fifteen inches, including the weight of his body, all by itself. It was at this moment that he recalled the spilled books of three weeks earlier. He realized that it would have had to be a very strong wind to blow through his bedroom and blow the books off of his dresser. In fact, he now realized that because the books fell toward the open

79

window, it was highly unlikely that they were toppled by the wind. Three days later, Ryan was sitting in the chair in his bedroom reading from a book of poems by Lord Byron, when the pole lamp fell across the right hand side of his chair, resting abruptly on the floor along the side of his chair. The lampshade, dented and crumpled from the fall, lay just inches from his right foot. Leaping from the chair, Ryan stood over the mysterious lamp astonished by the event.

"What do you think is going on?" Ryan was asking his mother.

Ryan had related all three of the strange incidents and was seeking some plausible explanation from his mother.

"Could be that you have an angelic visitor." Amelda displayed a weak smile and she used her best folksy voice for this most unexpected revelation.

"You mean I gotta ghost?" Ryan's jaw remained dropped and his mouth remained opened.

"Well...no. I think it's more like a spirit or angel." She said.

"Come on, Mom. You don't believe in angels and neither do I".

"I'm only suggesting that it's the only explanation that I can come up with, right now. You have to have an open mind on these things."

Ryan knew that she was only half kidding. He also knew, in spite of her playful notion, that she was experiencing a lot of pain lately. He could see it in her eyes more than anything. The incidence of angina pain in her chest was ever-increasing and her arthritis was becoming unbearable. She did her best to mask her ever-increasing discomfort from her husband and son. It was, however, difficult to hide the extreme pain she was now experiencing. Her daily activities were dramatically reduced. Especially, those involved with helping Josh with the actual farming. Her greatest fear, now, was her inability to manage her inside chores. The arthritic pain in her hands rendered the simple task of washing dishes impossible. Much of her time was now spent in a frantic state of worry of what the future held for her capacity as a wife and mother. She could feel her situation declining day by day. She must remain strong. At least, as strong as she could. There was so much left to do. There was so much more to accomplish, both as a mother and a wife. She would find a way. She just had to find a way.

Christmas morning found Ryan sitting in his chair beside his bed. It was nine-forty. Ryan was not feeling terribly cheerful. He sat staring out of his window. Thinking and wondering what was next. His mother lay in her bed, unable to move her legs or her hands due to the extreme state of her arthritis. Her angina was present almost all of the time. Finally, Amelda conjured up the stamina to call out to Ryan.

Not a scream, but loud enough for Ryan to hear, "Ryan, come talk with me."

Ryan entered her room. He moved quietly and slowly to the chair beside her bed. He couldn't bring himself to look at her. The pained and strained eyes were more than he could tolerate, for the moment. This would come soon enough.

"Don't you think that it's time that you wished your mother a merry Christmas?" she scowled, mockingly.

"I would feel better about Christmas if you could come downstairs."

"Ryan, you know that isn't going to happen. Now just sit with me for bit. I want to talk to you." That familiar half smile was there, but there was no sparkle in those thirty-eight year old eyes.

Finally, Ryan could look into her eyes. He could see the pain. He could also see the love and looking at her was now tolerable.

"Listen, my man, I have a solution to the aggravating angel problem." She sounded quite serious. "I'm going to get rid of him for you when I become an angel."

"Mom, don't talk like that. You won't become an angel for some time. Anyway, according to Lord Byron, angels don't do much."

"Meaning what?" Her suspicious nature, aroused.

"Well, I was reading a poem by Byron. It's called 'The Vision of Judgment'. There's this stanza that goes like this,"

'The Angels were all singing out of tune,

And hoarse with having little else to do,

Excepting to wind up the sun and moon

Or curb a runaway young star or two.'

"Oh that's just what angels do in their spare time. Other times they're doing all kinds of chores. Chores that help people, especially those people that they love. When it's my time to leave you, I will find a way to get rid of this *'pain-in-the-neck'* angel. After I accomplish that little task, I will take my turn winding up the sun." She pretended to take a smug pose, jutting out her lower lip.

Ryan smiled at her. He had never before felt so close and felt such love. "I'm going to get your Christmas present. Don't go away."

"No," she laughed lightly, "I'll be right here."

Exactly six weeks later, on February fifth, Amelda Palmer was dead.

A severe heart attack brought on by the arterial blockage near her heart signalled the end of her long journey and battle with pain and disappointment. Her worries were over. Josh and Ryan could barely cope with her demise. Ryan was determined to spend the rest of his life making her proud of him. Josh would last another thirteen years. He would never fully recover from the sense of loss.

[1]Lord Byron (1788-1824), English poet. The Vision of Judgement, st. 2

Ryan would remain with his father on the farm for another five years before moving to the small town some eleven miles from the farm. In the five years that they shared the farmhouse without Amelda, the two would never discuss their feelings about each other or Amelda's passing.

No headstone marked Amelda's grave on the day of her funeral. Ryan would work for another two months sculpting a remarkable likeness of his mother on a large granite stone that would eventually mark the place of her resting. His determination and devotion to purpose was absolute. Once finished, the granite stone portrayed his mother's face. Angel's wings could be noted in the background of the image. At sixteen, Ryan showed astonishing skill. It would be his last work of art. He couldn't bring himself to work at any more writing or sculpting. There was simply no motivation left that would drive him to such an accomplishment. The poetry and sculpting that he once loved simply held no purpose. He would find a way to find a life that his mother would be proud of. A life of sculpting and poems smacked too much of that of a hippie or welfare bum. He would find a way to do better.

Ryan would now prepare himself for the next amazing journey of his young life.

Thirteen Years Later

Ryan slumped in the chair of his living room, exhausted from three and a half hours of packing. Finally the job was complete. He was preparing to move back to his parents' farm after spending the last eight years in town. He had a small bungalow, one block off of the main street of this small town of seven hundred people. The entire eight years had been spent working for the bank as assistant manager. His prime duty was the management of the mortgage department.

He had married Debra one year after his arrival in town. They enjoyed a brief courtship of only five months and married happily. Debra gave birth to their daughter one year and three days after their wedding. Mel quickly became the light of Ryan's life. She was named for Ryan's mother and quickly adopted the shortened version of Mel. Debra and Ryan enjoyed a happy and calm life from the very outset. Their reputation for being extraordinarily content was widespread. They both doted on Mel, to the point of spoiling her, somewhat.

Tragedy struck in Mel's fourth year. While visiting Josh at the farm, Debra was driving the car back into town to pick up some clothing for Mel that they had forgotten. In a hard driving rain, she approached the wooden bridge that crossed the river that separated the farm from the town. Later speculation was that she approached the upgrade to the bridge at a speed that rendered her airborne, crashing through the flimsy wooden side rail and smashing into the cold water of the river. The current was strong and she may have been unconscious due to the impact. Debra was discovered approximately two hours later by a passing vehicle. Death was due to drowning. As the car remained imbedded in the river bottom, the water line had reached some three inches from the roof of the car enabling the rushing water to fill the car, quickly, through the broken window.

Devastated, Ryan and Mel grieved for many months. Returning to town, Ryan resumed his work at the bank. He had a middle aged lady, the wife of one of his co-workers, come to his house each day to care for Mel until the following year when she started school. He devoted himself to Mel and her well being to the exclusion of any further romantic endeavours or pursuits. Mel, on the other hand, grieved quickly as is normal for a four or five year old. She was likely aware of her loss, however, not likely aware of its lasting effects.

And now, as Ryan finished his packing and prepared for the return to the farm, he reflected on his third and most recent tragic loss. Josh Palmer had died just six weeks ago and three days short of his fifty-fifth birthday. The end came with a sharp piercing pain to the back of his skull as a severe brain aneurysm ripped from him his intellect, his loving nature and finally, his life. Ryan would now, forever, forego any closure or explanation of Josh's lack of ability to communicate, to his only child, the love and admiration that he felt. He could, at least, derive a sense of contentment with the thought that his father would now join his mother in her angelic pursuits, whether doing their angel chores or winding up the sun.

Back at the farm, Ryan would commute daily, the short trek into town to his job. Mel, now seven, would busy herself during the day at school and both had found a reasonably happy life...quiet as it was.

Shortly after moving back to the farm, Ryan had hired a man to tend the vegetables. The farm was virtually halved for growing purposes and quite manageable for one knowledgeable and hard workingman. Ryan was in such a hurry to make the hire; he didn't take the time to thoroughly check-out Clinton Harding. He was quiet, almost shy. But he seemed to know about vegetables and farming. He said that he had farmed for a number of years a couple of hundred miles south west of the area. Ryan decided to depend on his first impression and give Clinton the opportunity.

It was only a matter of a few weeks before Ryan came to dreadfully regret his cloudy insight and quick decision. Arriving home from work at four fifteen, Ryan found the farmhouse empty. Mel would catch the school bus in the schoolyard at twenty to four and arrive home at about four-ten. It was easier for Ryan to arrive home five minutes after Mel, rather than have her wait in the schoolyard for thirty minutes before he could pick her up. This was pretty common practice in this small town and rural setting. He usually came through the front door to the leaping, hugging enthusiasm of his daughter. Then, and only then, was she allowed to go outside to play until dinner. Ryan's first reaction to the empty home was one of annoyance at the notion that Mel had 'broken the rules' by going outside prior to his arrival. Moving through the house to the back door, Ryan stepped outside to the back stoop.

"Mel", he called, "you out here?"

There was no response and a quick glance in all directions started a small panic in the pit of Ryan's stomach. He moved towards the barn, half running. The large wooden doors were open. As he entered, he expected to find Clinton, if not Mel. Again, his quick look in all directions of the barn deepened his queasy upset.

"Clinton...Mel!" he almost screamed. Suddenly he knew there would be no response. He didn't know why he knew. He simply knew. In a panic driven scurry, he combed the entire house, the barn and the property, knowing all along that his search would be in vain.

At ten minutes after midnight, the two policemen and the dozen or so townspeople decided to leave Ryan's living room and gather again in the morning at the outdoor café on the main street in town. From that point they would split into teams and begin a thorough search of all wooded and heavily bushed areas. Ryan remained speechless as they left the house offering encouragement and assurances that all would end well.

Once alone, Ryan retired to his bed. He didn't bother undressing. He simply lay on the top of the neatly made bed. Eyes open.

And so began his longest and most painful journey.

Four police officers and twenty-eight townspeople joined Ryan at the main street café. Ryan gave over to the police chief for supervision of the search. Each policeman gathered seven people for their search team. Ryan joined the group that was going to search near the farm. It was seven-forty in the morning when the four teams split up and began their search.

Ryan's team arrived at the wooded area bordering the eastern edge of his farm property a couple of minutes before eight a.m. They formed a single line with approximately twenty-five feet between them. They turned into the wooded area, moving slowly and intently. Ryan could not keep the strangest thoughts from his wandering mind. He caught himself evaluating the odds that, of all thirty-three people taking part in the search, he would find his daughter. He had concluded that the odds were astronomically against him being the one to discover Mel. He had no sooner brushed this notion from his mind when he caught himself assuming that if Mel was found in a wooded area, the chances that she would be alive were minuscule. On and on it went for some forty minutes. Suddenly, he could hear police Chief Atkinson calling his name.

"Ryan! Ryan!" the shouts were getting closer by the second. Chief Atkinson finally appeared through an opening in the trees. Smiling broadly, the chief spoke words from heaven. All four policemen were carrying cellular telephones for the purpose of communication between the teams. The chief had received the call from the team in town. They hadn't left for the search area when the good news was discovered.

"They've found her...in town. She's alright."

"Let's go." Ryan spoke as calmly and evenly as he could. He had never before experienced such emotion. His heart and stomach had reversed places. His head was spinning out of control and his eyes burned from holding back his tears.

There was a crowd of people standing on the sidewalk portion of the café. Ryan's car came to a stop at the curb. He burst out of the car and could see Mel's sweet but pale face smiling at him through the throng of happy searchers.

Just as the last search team was about to depart, two members called out and up the main street at the figure of a small girl walking slowly yet directly toward them. It was Mel. She had approached from the north end of the street where a left turn put you into a thicket of brush and trees. She was in need of a good washing and she could use a little more colour in her cheeks. However, she was not physically hurt in any way. She was hungry and wanted desperately to see her father.

She now explained her journey to her father and the crowd of happy and curious onlookers.

"Clinton took me for a walk, last night. But it was too long and I got tired. I slept on a pile of leaves by a tree. When I woke up this morning I asked Clinton if we could go home. Then I got scared 'cause he didn't look right and he started to talk funny."

"What did he want? Where was he going?" Ryan asked, almost panicked.

"I don't know. Then he sat on the ground and told me to go to town and leave him alone."

"Did he hurt you or touch you in any way?" Chief Atkinson asked deliberately.

"No...he just said that I should leave him alone."

"How did you find your way through the woods to the street, honey?" Ryan was talking a mile a second.

"I was going to tell you, daddy. You're going too fast." Mel's eyes welled up.

"Okay...Okay, honey. What happened?" he lowered his voice.

"Well, after a couple of feet, a lady showed me the way out and followed me until I got to the street."

"What lady? Who is she? Do you know her?" once again Ryan's voice was speeding.

"No, daddy. When I turned to say thank you, she was gone."

"Probably, someone in cahoots with Clinton" surmised Chief Atkinson.

All present started toward the wooded area at the north end of town. They were only about a hundred and fifty feet into the woods when they found Clinton. It quickly became obvious what Clinton had done. He had threaded a half-inch rope through the buckle of his heavy, black and leather belt tying it around a branch some eighteen feet up off of the ground. The belt had been securely tightened around his neck. He had likely climbed the tree and out onto the branch, jumping so as to hang himself. There was Clinton, as still and as dead as can be. They would never know what drove him to his harmless hike with Mel or what drove his decision to commit suicide.

"We're not likely to find his female friend around. She's probably several miles away by now." proclaimed Chief Atkinson.

Three weeks had passed since Mel's fifteen hours of terror. Ryan had decided that it was time that Mel paid her first visit to her grandmother's grave. They would leave a few flowers and the visit would give them an opportunity to talk about Amelda. Ryan hadn't told Mel very much about his mother, to this point. It seemed to him that it was time that Mel understood who and how wonderful her grandmother was.

As they both knelt in front of the large granite headstone, Mel looked up at the two and a half foot high, carved likeness of her grandmother. Slowly, she turned to her father.

"Hey, daddy. That's the nice lady that helped me in the woods with Clinton."

Ryan froze, staring at his seven year-old daughter. Finally, a gradual smile came over his lips. He had, just this moment, recalled that there were no more incidents of falling books or lamps in the old farmhouse after his mother's death.

"Your grandmother is busy these days, winding up the sun."

CPSIA information can be obtained at www.ICGtesting.com
Printed in the USA
LVOW06s1828280314

379396LV00001B/91/P